Dear Parent:
Your child's love of reading starts here!

Every child learns to read in a different way and at his or her own speed. Some go back and forth between reading levels and read favorite books again and again. Others read through each level in order. You can help your young reader improve and become more confident by encouraging his or her own interests and abilities. From books your child reads with you to the first books he or she reads alone, there are I Can Read Books for every stage of reading:

SHARED READING
Basic language, word repetition, and whimsical illustrations, ideal for sharing with your emergent reader

BEGINNING READING
Short sentences, familiar words, and simple concepts for children eager to read on their own

READING WITH HELP
Engaging stories, longer sentences, and language play for developing readers

READING ALONE
Complex plots, challenging vocabulary, and high-interest topics for the independent reader

ADVANCED READING
Short paragraphs, chapters, and exciting themes for the perfect bridge to chapter books

I Can Read Books have introduced children to the joy of reading since 1957. Featuring award-winning authors and illustrators and a fabulous cast of beloved characters, I Can Read Books set the standard for beginning readers.

A lifetime of discovery begins with the magical words "I Can Read!"

Visit www.icanread.com for information
on enriching your child's reading experience.

Biscuit
Treasury

by ALYSSA SATIN CAPUCILLI

pictures by PAT SCHORIES

I Can Read® is a trademark of HarperCollins Publishers.

Biscuit Treasury

Biscuit
Text copyright © 1996 by Alyssa Satin Capucilli
Illustrations copyright © 1996 by Pat Schories

Bathtime for Biscuit
Text copyright © 1998 by Alyssa Satin Capucilli
Illustrations copyright © 1998 by Pat Schories

Biscuit Goes to School
Text copyright © 2002 by Alyssa Satin Capucilli
Illustrations copyright © 2002 by Pat Schories

Biscuit's Day at the Farm
Text copyright © 2007 by Alyssa Satin Capucilli
Illustrations copyright © 2007 by Pat Schories

Biscuit Loves the Library
Text copyright © 2014 by Alyssa Satin Capucilli
Illustrations copyright © 2014 by Pat Schories

Biscuit Feeds the Pets
Text copyright © 2016 by Alyssa Satin Capucilli
Illustrations copyright © 2016 by Pat Schories

For information address HarperCollins Children's Books, a division of
HarperCollins Publishers, 195 Broadway, New York, NY 10007
www.harpercollinschildrens.com
ISBN 978-0-06-285332-5
18 19 20 21 22 SCP 10 9 8 7 6 5 4 3 2 1
First Edition

Biscuit
Treasury

HARPER
An Imprint of HarperCollinsPublishers

Table of Contents

Biscuit

story by ALYSSA SATIN CAPUCILLI
pictures by PAT SCHORIES

For Laura and Peter who wait patiently
for a Biscuit of their very own
—A. S. C.

For Tess
—P. S.

This is Biscuit.

Biscuit is small.

Biscuit is yellow.

Time for bed, Biscuit!

Woof, woof!

Biscuit wants to play.

Time for bed, Biscuit!

Woof, woof!

Biscuit wants a snack.

Time for bed, Biscuit!

Woof, woof!

Biscuit wants a drink.

Time for bed, Biscuit!

Woof, woof!

Biscuit wants to hear a story.

Time for bed, Biscuit!

Woof, woof!

Biscuit wants his blanket.

Time for bed, Biscuit!

Woof, woof!

Biscuit wants his doll.

Time for bed, Biscuit!

Woof, woof!

Biscuit wants a hug.

Time for bed, Biscuit!

Woof, woof!

Biscuit wants a kiss.

Time for bed, Biscuit!

Woof, woof!

Biscuit wants a light on.

Woof!

Biscuit wants to be tucked in.

Woof!

Biscuit wants one more kiss.

Woof!

Biscuit wants one more hug.

Woof!

Biscuit wants to curl up.

Sleepy puppy.

Good night, Biscuit.

Bathtime for Biscuit

story by ALYSSA SATIN CAPUCILLI
pictures by PAT SCHORIES

This one is for my parents.
—A.S.C.

To Sri K.
—P.S.

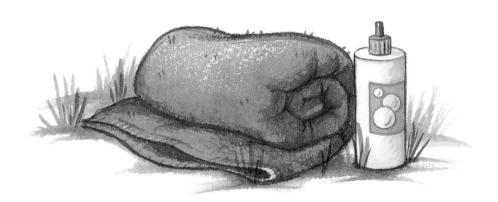

Time for a bath, Biscuit!

Woof, woof!

Biscuit wants to play.

Time for a bath, Biscuit!

Woof, woof!

Biscuit wants to dig.

Time for a bath, Biscuit!

Woof, woof!

Biscuit wants to roll.

Time for a bath, Biscuit!

Time to get nice and clean.

Woof, woof!

In you go!

Woof!

Biscuit does not want a bath!

Bow wow!
Biscuit sees
his friend Puddles.

Woof, woof!

Biscuit wants to climb out.

Come back, Biscuit!

Woof!

Come back, Puddles!

Bow wow!

Biscuit and Puddles
want to play
in the sprinkler.

Biscuit and Puddles
want to dig
in the mud.

Biscuit and Puddles
want to roll
in the flower bed.

Now I have you!

Woof, woof!

Let go of the towel,

Biscuit!

Bow wow!
Let go of the towel,
Puddles!

Silly puppies!

Let go!

Woof, woof!
Bow wow!

Oh!

Time for a bath, Biscuit!

Woof, woof!

A bath for all of us!

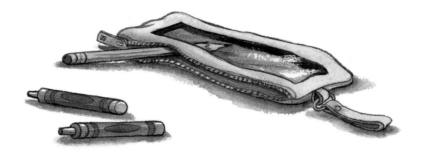

Biscuit
Goes to School

story by ALYSSA SATIN CAPUCILLI
pictures by PAT SCHORIES

*For the wonderful students, teachers,
librarians, and parents who have
welcomed Biscuit into their schools!*

Here comes the school bus!
Woof, woof!

Stay here, Biscuit.

Dogs don't go to school.

Woof!

Where is Biscuit going?

Is Biscuit going to the pond?

Woof!

Is Biscuit going to the park?
Woof!

Biscuit is going to school!
Woof, woof!

Biscuit wants to play ball.

Woof, woof!

Biscuit wants
to hear a story.
Woof, woof!
Shhh!

Biscuit wants a snack.

Woof, woof!

Oh, Biscuit!

What are you doing here?

Dogs don't go to school!

Oh, no!

Here comes the teacher!

Woof!

Biscuit wants
to meet the teacher.
Woof!

Biscuit wants
to meet the class.
Woof, woof!

Biscuit likes school!

Woof, woof!

And everyone at school
likes Biscuit!
Woof!

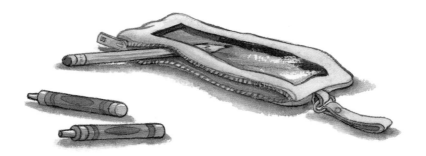

For Daniel William and Adam Joshua,
brothers and best friends!
—A.S.C.

Biscuit's
Day at the Farm

story by ALYSSA SATIN CAPUCILLI
pictures by PAT SCHORIES

Come along, Biscuit.
We're going to help
on the farm today.

Woof, woof!

We can feed the hens, Biscuit.

Woof, woof!

We can feed the pigs, too.

The pigpen
is empty, Biscuit.
Where can the pigs be?

Woof, woof!

Funny puppy.

You found the pig
and the piglets, too.
Woof!

Let's feed the goats,
Biscuit.
Woof, woof!

Oink!

Oh, Biscuit.

The piglet is out of the pen.

We must put
the piglet back.
Woof, woof!

Let's feed the sheep, Biscuit.
Woof, woof!

Oink!

Oh no, Biscuit.

It's the piglet!

We must put the piglet back
one more time.
Woof, woof!

Here are the geese,
Biscuit.

Woof, woof!

Oink!

Here is the piglet again.

Woof, woof!

Oink! Oink!

Honk!

Wait, Biscuit!
The geese are just
saying hello.

Woof!

Silly puppy!
The piglet is back
in the pen.

And so are you, Biscuit!

Oink!

Woof, woof!

*For Elliot Jude Chaplin,
and for our beloved librarian
friends who share the love of
reading with all of us!
—A.S.C. and P.S.*

Biscuit Loves the Library

story by ALYSSA SATIN CAPUCILLI
pictures by PAT SCHORIES

It's a very special day
at the library, Biscuit.
Woof, woof!

It's Read to a Pet Day!

I can read to you,

Biscuit.

Woof, woof!

Come along, Biscuit.

Let's find a book.

Woof, woof!

See, Biscuit?
There are books
about bunnies and bears.
Woof, woof!

And big dinosaurs, too!

Woof!

Funny puppy!

That's not a real bone!

Woof, woof!

Look, Biscuit.

There are more books

over here.

Woof, woof!

Biscuit! Where are you?

Woof!

You found the puppets,
Biscuit.

Woof, woof!
And you even found
stories we can listen to.
Woof!

Now, which book will it be?

Woof, woof!

Biscuit! Wait for me!

Woof!

Oh, Biscuit!

You found the librarian
and a book that's just right.
Woof, woof!

You found a cozy spot

filled with friends, too.

Everyone loves the library,
Biscuit.
Woof, woof!

Let's read!

Woof!

For James, who loves to help
feed the pets!
—A.S.C.

Biscuit Feeds the Pets

story by ALYSSA SATIN CAPUCILLI
pictures by PAT SCHORIES

Here, Biscuit.

We're going to help

Mrs. Gray today.

Woof, woof!

We're going to help
feed the pets!

Are you ready, Biscuit?

Woof, woof!

We can help feed
the fish, Biscuit.

We can help feed
the kittens, too.
Woof, woof!
Meow!

Wait, Biscuit!

Where are you going?

Woof, woof!
Yip—yip—yip!

Oh, Biscuit.

You found the new puppies!

Woof!

This way, Biscuit.

Woof, woof!

There are more pets
to feed over here.

Woof!

Biscuit!

Come out of there.

It's not time to play.

It's time to help Mrs. Gray.

Woof!

Yip!

Oh no, Biscuit!

Come back.

How will we feed

the pets now?

Woof, woof!

Yip—yip—yip!

Meow!

No, Biscuit, no.

Not the water bowl!

SPLASH!

Silly puppies!

Woof, woof!
Yip—yip—yip!

Funny puppy!

You found your own way to
help feed the pets, Biscuit.

You made lots of
new friends, too!

Meow!

Yip—yip—yip!

Woof, woof!

Biscuit